The
BIG GREEN BOOK

ROBERT GRAVES

The

BIG GREEN BOOK

Illustrated by

MAURICE SENDAK

Macmillan Publishing Company

New York

Copyright © 1962 by Robert Graves
Copyright © 1962 by Maurice Sendak

Macmillan Publishing Company
866 Third Avenue, New York, N.Y. 10022
Collier Macmillan Canada, Inc.

First Crowell-Collier Press edition 1962;
reissued in new format 1968; reissued in original
format by Macmillan Publishing Company 1985

Printed in the United States of America

10 9 8 7 6 5 4 3 2 1

Library of Congress Cataloging in Publication Data
Graves, Robert, date.
The big green book.

Reprint. Originally published: New York:
Crowell-Collier, 1962.
Summary: A little boy finds a big green book in the
attic and learns many handy magic spells that he uses
with surprising results.
1 Children's stories, English. [1. Magic—Fiction.
2. Orphans—Fiction. 3. Aunts—Fiction. 4. Uncles—
Fiction] I. Sendak, Maurice, ill. II. Title.
PZ7.G77525Bi 1985 [Fic] 84-42972
ISBN 0-02-736810-6

Long ago a little boy called Jack lived with his uncle
and his aunt and a big dog (who used to chase rabbits)
in a house among the fields.

Jack's father and mother were dead, and the uncle and aunt were not very nice to him. What Jack didn't at all like was when the uncle and aunt took him for nice long walks in the fields, instead of letting him go out alone with the dog.

One day he went to play in the attic of his house,
and there he found a big green book hidden under an
old sack in a corner.

Jack took up the big green book and began to read
it. He hoped it was a story book; but he found it was
something far better.

His eyes got bigger and bigger as he read. The big green book was full of magic spells. It told him how to make himself as old or young as he liked, and how to change the look of things, and how to make birds or animals do just as he liked, and how to disappear. At the end there were spells for winning card games, and for learning lessons just by looking at them for a moment.

I can't tell you *how* all these things were done, because this was a long time ago, and the big green book of magic has now disappeared too. But most of the spells in books of this sort begin with: "First you make a magic circle around you with a long stick, then you take three deep breaths..."

Jack hid the big green book under his shirt and went out of the house to read it in a field beyond the garden. He sat down and said to himself: "I had better change into an old man first, so that if my uncle and aunt see me they won't ask: 'What is that big green book you have there?'" So he made a circle around himself with a long stick, took three deep breaths, and read one of the magic spells out of the book.

Soon he found he was not a little boy any more—he was an old man with a long beard.

But because he still had on his own clothes, he said another spell and changed them into rags, so that if his uncle and aunt came by they would not know who he was.

He went on reading and reading in the big green book, and trying all the magic spells, and having great fun.

The aunt wanted to take Jack for a nice long walk
that day. She looked for him in the attic, but he was
not to be found;

and then in the garden, but he was not to be found;

and she called, but he did not come.

So she and the uncle went to look for him in the fields, but he was not to be found in the fields.

When they went up to the attic window and looked all around for miles, they could see no one but a ragged old man sitting in a field beyond the garden. He was reading a big green book.

The aunt said to the uncle: "We must ask that ragged old man if he has seen Jack anywhere."

"We will," said the uncle.

So they took the dog (who used to chase rabbits)
out of the house, and went through the garden into
the field.

As they came up, the ragged old man (who was really Jack all the time) hid the big green book under his rags and said a spell to make himself disappear.

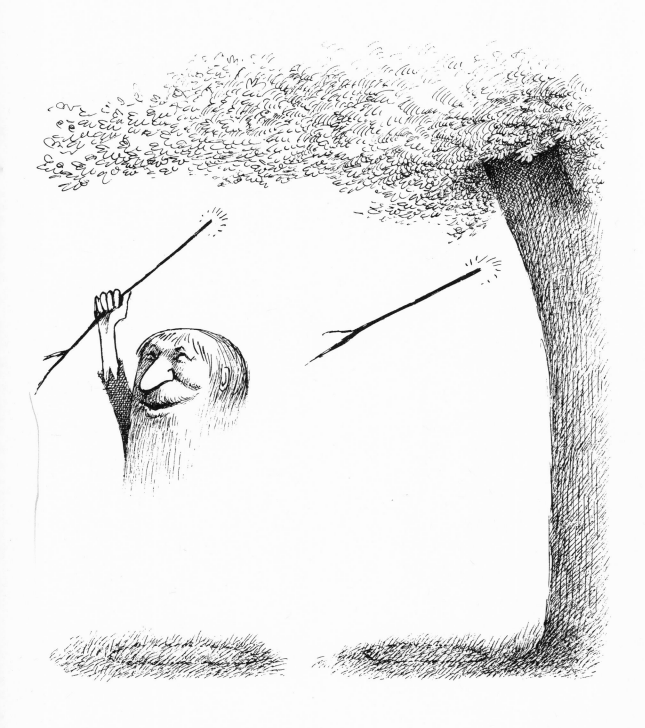

The uncle said to the aunt: "I saw an old man, didn't you? But he has disappeared."

Jack went behind them quietly and then took off the spell, so that he could be seen again. Then he said: "Good morning!" They turned round and said: "Old man, there you are! Have you seen a little boy anywhere?"

Jack began to laugh.

"Why do you laugh, old man?" asked the uncle.

Jack said: "It was such a funny thing to ask me. Yes: a little boy was here only a minute ago. He said his name was Jack. Now he's disappeared."

"Thank you very much, old man," said the uncle
and aunt. "We must go and look for him."

"Stop and have a game of cards with me first," said
Jack. He now knew all the magic spells for winning
games, and he had used another spell for turning some
old dead leaves into a pack of cards.

The uncle and aunt said: "Very well. We will play
against you for a dollar a game."

They then sat down in the field and began to play
cards with Jack. They lost the game.

The next time they played for two dollars a game, and lost;

and next time they played for four dollars and lost;

and the next time for eight dollars a game and lost.

Each time they were sure that they would win everything back, and doubled the dollars, but they always
lost, until they owed Jack about a hundred thousand
dollars.

"That's enough," said Jack. "I'm too lucky for you. Pay me the hundred thousand dollars, and we can stop playing."

"Give us only one more game!" said the uncle. "I'm
sure I'll win everything back this time if you double
the dollars again."

When he lost the game the uncle said: "We should never have played cards against you, old man. You are so lucky. And now we have no more dollars left. But give us one more chance, and if we lose this game you can have our house and garden, and our dog who chases rabbits, and everything else."

"Yes, give us another chance," said the aunt.

"Very well," said Jack. They played another game, and again the uncle lost.

Then the uncle and aunt said: "One last game, old man! Then either you give us back the money and the house and the garden and the dog who chases rabbits, and everything else, or we will be your servants for the rest of our lives."

"Very well," said Jack; and they played again, and lost again.

"We are your servants for the rest of our lives," said the uncle and aunt. "Now what will happen to poor little Jack?"

"Well," said Jack, "the first thing is to find him, and then we can think what to do with him. I may like the little boy. I may let him stay on in the house. Take me there!"

"Old man," said the aunt, "first tell us how you managed to win the game every time."

"Oh, just by magic," said Jack, throwing away the cards, which turned back into dead old leaves.

"How wonderful!" said the uncle. "Show me some more magic!"

"Well," said Jack, "you see these three green peas? I took them from your garden. Put them in a row in the middle of your hand, and see if you can blow the middle one away without blowing away the outside ones!"

The uncle tried, but he could not blow away the middle one without blowing away the others too.

"This is how you do it!" said Jack. He bent down
two fingers to hold the two outside peas in place, and
then he blew away the middle pea.

"Oh, that isn't magic!" said the uncle. "I can do it myself."

"Try!" said Jack. "Here are the three peas."

The uncle put the three peas in a row in the middle of his hand, but when he bent down his fingers to hold the outside peas, Jack said a spell and the uncle's fingernails grew longer and longer and went right through his hand.

"Ow!" said the uncle. "My fingernails have grown through my hand!"

Jack laughed and laughed; but he made the nails grow short and come out again from his uncle's hand.

As they went home, the dog chased a rabbit.

"He is always chasing rabbits," said the uncle.
"Often we have rabbit pie."

"Well, there will be no rabbit pie today," said Jack. He made another spell, and the rabbit which was being chased turned round and hit the dog hard on the nose. The dog ran away, and the rabbit chased him across the fields until they both disappeared.

Jack laughed, and the aunt laughed, and the uncle laughed, and then they all went back through the garden to the door of the house.

"This house is all yours, old man," said the uncle.
"The garden too."

"Very well, let me go inside the house and have a
look," said Jack.

He went inside, changed back into a little boy, clothes and all, put the big green book back under the sack in the attic, and came down again.

"Oh, there you are at last, Jack!" said the uncle and aunt. "This house and garden are not ours any more, I'm sorry to say; and we are both servants for the rest of our lives. We played cards with a ragged old man and lost everything!"

"Oh, uncle, you always told *me* not to play cards for money," said Jack. "Now, what will you do? And what will become of me?"

"The ragged old man will be nice to you, I hope," said the aunt. "He has just gone into the house to look at it. It is *his* house now."

"I saw no ragged old man," said Jack. "You must be dreaming! And, tell me, where's our dog?"

"Oh, the dog got chased by a rabbit," said the aunt.

"Now I *know* you must be dreaming," said Jack. "Rabbits don't chase dogs."

"This one did," said the aunt.

She and the uncle then went into the house, but
the ragged old man was not to be found anywhere.

They felt very silly.

"You are right, Jack," said the aunt, "we must have been dreaming. We are not the ragged old man's servants after all, because there was no ragged old man. And all our dollars and this house and garden are still ours!"

Jack laughed and laughed. But he never told them
what he had done, ever.

He was rather scared of what he could do with the
big green book.

So he used only the spell which let him learn by just looking at the lessons for a moment. He was always top of his class.

But the dog was now so scared of rabbits that they
never had rabbit pie again in that house, ever!